Tashi

and the
WICKED MAGICIAN
and other stories

Tashi

and the
WICKED MAGICIAN
and other stories

ANNA FIENBERG
and
BARBARA FIENBERG

pictures by
GEOFF KELLY *and* KIM GAMBLE

ALLEN&UNWIN
SYDNEY · MELBOURNE · AUCKLAND · LONDON

First published in 2014

Allen & Unwin
83 Alexander Street
Crows Nest NSW 2065
Australia
Phone: (61 2) 8425 0100
Email: info@allenandunwin.com
Web: www.allenandunwin.com

A Cataloguing-in-Publication entry is available
from the National Library of Australia
www.trove.nla.gov.au

ISBN 978 174331 508 8

Cover and text design by Sandra Nobes
Cover and text illustrations by Geoff Kelly
Set in 15 pt Horley Old Style by Sandra Nobes
Colour reproduction by Splitting Image, Clayton, Victoria.
This book was printed in July 2014 at Hang Tai Printing (Guang Dong) Ltd.,
Xin Cheng Ind Est, Xie Gang Town, Dong Guan, Guang Dong Province, China

10 9 8 7 6 5 4 3 2 1

Contents

Tashi and the Wicked Magician ~ 1

Tashi and the Burning House ~ 20

Tashi and the Orchid Thieves ~ 37

Tashi the Brave, Part One ~ 57

Part Two, Face to Face ~ 73

For Len, with love,

AF & BF

TASHI AND THE
WICKED MAGICIAN

'HEY, TASHI,' CALLED Jack. 'Wait!'

Tashi stopped, and turned.

Jack was panting when he caught up. 'Ask me for five dollars.'

'I don't need any money, thanks,' Tashi patted his bag. 'I've brought my lunch today. And we'd better hurry – we'll be late for school.' He looked at Jack's eyebrows still waggling mysteriously. 'Oh, I see…Jack, could you lend me five dollars?'

'Sure,' said Jack, and he whipped out a shiny black wallet from his back pocket.

Tashi put out his hand to feel the leather, just as Jack opened it. '*Wah!*' Tall bright flames shot up, making Tashi snatch back his hand.

Quick as a slap, Jack snapped the wallet closed, snuffing out the flames. It lay there in his palm, quiet.

Tashi took it carefully, and sniffed it.

Jack grinned. 'Have a look inside. But open it slowly.'

Tashi peered in, and scratched his head.

'Magic, hey? Look closer – there's a secret metal pocket, and when you snap it open, it triggers a spark. Isn't it mad? Uncle Joe gave it to me.'

'Where did he get it?'

'India. And he saw a magician do a trick with a rope that uncoils by itself and stretches straight up into the sky. Totally mysterious.'

As the boys entered the playground, the bell rang.

'Magic is very fascinating but it can also be very dangerous,' said Tashi.

'The Ancient Egyptians believed in magic,' said Angus Figment, following them into class. 'When babies were sick, their mothers were told to eat a mouse for good luck and put the bones in a bag to hang around the baby's neck.'

'Erk,' said Jack. 'So, have you ever met a magician, Tashi?'

Tashi nodded slowly. 'I've met a few in my time. Most were clever, good men. But one...' Tashi shuddered and looked away.

'One?' said Jack and Angus.

'Later,' said Tashi, pointing to Ms Hall, who'd just started the lesson.

At recess, the boys sat on the bench under the peppercorn tree. 'So,' said Jack, 'tell us about the One.'

Tashi opened his egg noodles, then leaned back and closed his eyes, remembering. 'Well,' he sighed, 'it was like this. One morning when I was down in the village square, I saw a crowd of people gathered in front of the posters on the wall where we read the news.'

'What, like a big internet screen?' said Angus.

Tashi looked puzzled. 'No, like newspapers. Each week the papers are stuck up on the wall for everyone to read. In my village, not *everyone* can buy a newspaper! But I could see it wasn't the news that was causing such an excited buzz that day.'

'Well, what?' asked Angus.

'There were too many people blocking my view for me to read what it was all about, so I had to use my elbows and knees and feet to wriggle clear until finally I got to the front of the crowd.

'And now I could see: it was a big poster, dramatic and striking. The top half was a picture of a turban, a cloak, trousers and shoes, but no person was inside them. Underneath was the message:

THE MAGNIFICENT MAGI IS COMING!
Don't miss the Magi, Supreme Master of Illusion
Coming to your village next week.
Two performances only.

'Well, everyone in the village wanted to go, but the tickets cost more than most people could afford. So you can imagine how pleased I was when Ah Chu's mother knocked on the door next day with some unexpected news.

'"Oh Tashi," she cried, "I've been wanting to thank you for saving my baby from that River Pirate, and now I've thought of a good way to do it. Can you guess?

I have sold a pig and bought tickets for our two families to see the Magi!"

'We thought it was a wonderful idea. Magic was all we talked about during the six days of waiting. My friends and I borrowed all the books on magic from the school library – there were only four – and tried magic tricks out on our families.'

'Did you learn how to make a rabbit jump out of a hat?' asked Angus. 'Or–'

'Levitate?' asked Jack. 'Uncle Joe said he saw a man in India sitting on air for half an hour, reading a book.'

'That's impossible,' said Angus.

'Is not,' said Jack. 'Uncle Joe saw it with his own eyes!'

'Not everything in this world is what it seems,' Tashi said. 'On the evening of the show we were all so excited, we decided to meet in the square so we could walk up to the schoolhouse together. Oh, but the grown-ups were so slow! Lotus Blossom, Ah Chu and I ran ahead and waited, and ran ahead and waited so many times. When we finally got to the hall it was almost full, just a few single seats left here and there. I was so disappointed.

'Then I looked again. The front row was empty!
It seems people were a bit nervous about sitting too
close to a magician – who knew what he might do?
He might turn them into a monkey! Quickly I waved to
our families, *hurry, hurry, down here!* and held my breath
until we were all safely seated.

'The lights went out, *ping*, and the empty stage was
lit by an eerie green glow. The Magi appeared out of a
puff of smoke and he held up his arms until the clapping
died down. Suddenly it was so quiet. Even Ah Chu's little
sister was hushed. The thrill in the air made my stomach
rumble. What would the Magi do next?

'A peacock suddenly flew out of the green-underwater
light, the silken sweep of its tail flashing before it
vanished. I blinked – it all happened so fast, it made me
wonder if I'd been dreaming.

'A sigh went up when a beautiful lady stepped out of a
cage. She bowed and danced a few steps, before
returning to it. A firecracker of blue smoke exploded, and
when the cage doors opened again, a white tiger sprang
out! I swung round to look at the Baron – for surely it
was *his* tiger – but he looked as astonished as anyone.

'The tiger advanced to the front of the stage. It stood staring out at us with its strange cat eyes. No one moved. It was so close, I could see a drop of saliva on its whisker. Next to me, Favourite Aunt clutched her purse, ready to run.

'"*Incanta!*" the Magi sang softly.

'The tiger turned to face him. Whole seconds passed, and neither of them blinked. The tension was unbearable. And then, like a disobedient pet that suddenly decides to behave, the tiger padded towards him. The Magi slung a rope around its neck like a leash, still chanting the word, and led the tiger back to the cage.

'When it was safely locked up, the Magi asked for a person in the audience to help him with his next act. No hands went up. I could hear people squirming on their seats, and Cousin Wu had such a fit of coughing that he had to go out. But the Magi looked along the rows of seats until his eyes dropped down to mine. He nodded, "This boy here, I think. Will you come up and help me?"

'My mother gave me a little push and I stumbled up to the stage, feeling a bit awkward and shy. When the Magi asked my name (and the audience cheered!)

I felt more comfortable. He tapped me on the head with his wand, spun me around three times and then, with a flourish, plucked a red rose from my ear. The audience gasped and cheered, but as I had turned to face him, I'd seen him slip the rose from his cuff.

'The Magi's eyes darkened, and locked on mine. He knew I had noticed. We held each other's gaze for a long moment until he dismissed me with a wave, "Thank you, Tashi."

'I lost track of the next few tricks. I know that a glass floated in the air by itself, a pitcher of water was filled many times over and never spilled, a solid ladder appeared out of nowhere. But it all wafted past in a blur, the wonder of it hardly touching me. I was still feeling the power and the menace of his eyes boring into mine. A shadow crept over me, and I felt a coldness deep inside my mind.

'Then a loud drum roll broke into my thoughts.

'"For my final illusion," the Magi said, "I would like another volunteer to join me on the stage – someone brave enough and ready to step into the unknown."

'Of course he couldn't have chosen better words to appeal to Lotus Blossom–'

'Oh yes!' cried Jack. 'I remember when she shouted at a *snake*, trying to scare it!'

Tashi nodded. 'She's brave, but she doesn't always think first before she acts.'

'You wouldn't have very long to think, though, if a snake was about to bite you,' Angus put in. 'So what did she do this time?'

'Well,' said Tashi, 'she put up her hand and waved frantically at the Magi. "That's me! Choose *me*!" she called.

'The Magi bowed and beckoned her to come onto the stage. Once she was beside him and had told him her name, he turned to the audience. "Now, with the help of a little hypnosis, we will find out how Lotus Blossom sees the world around her."

'He took off the glittering medal he wore on a golden chain around his neck and began to swing it before her eyes, murmuring to her all the while. He kept up the same slow rhythm, back and forth, back and forth, like a clock ticking. Lotus Blossom's shoulders slumped and her jaw dropped. She seemed to be asleep. She was in a trance!

'The Magi stepped back and said clearly, "You are the teacher of the village school in a classroom of children who are being very naughty. They are not listening to you and keep fooling around. How are you going to make them behave?"

'Lotus Blossom drew herself up and stood with her hands on her hips, shaking her head sadly. She was Teacher Pang! How could it be that she looked so exactly like our teacher! Then, in Mr Pang's voice, she said, "Hai Ping, what am I going to do with you? You are as bad as your father, you can never concentrate for more than two minutes at a time." The audience roared with laughter, but Lotus Blossom didn't hear them. She turned to her next pupils, the Wu brothers. "As for you boys, I see that you've been scribbling on the walls and throwing your books about again. Shame on you, I'll just have to–", but here the Magi stopped her by snapping his fingers. Perhaps he was a bit nervous about what she was going to say next. Anyway, Lotus Blossom jerked awake and became herself again. The audience clapped and cheered and gathered around her, laughing and congratulating her.

'On the way home, I questioned her about being hypnotised. She couldn't remember anything after telling the Magi her name. "Why? What did I do? What's wrong, Tashi?"

'"It's hard to explain," I told her. "It's just that – I feel very nervous about this man having such power over anyone. I think he could use it to cause harm."

'"But it was *fun*," she burst out, her lip pouting. "How do you know he's bad?"

'"I just know," I said.

'And that is why, the next night, I waited outside the schoolhouse after the second show and secretly followed the Magi when he left the building. The Baron was with him – he must have been waiting too – and together they walked back to the Baron's house where the Magi was staying.

'I knelt on a bench outside the Baron's library window, listening while the two men had a drink. Then, as the Baron drained his glass and made for the door, the Magi called him back. He was holding his golden chain again, swinging the medal before the Baron's eyes. I saw the Baron's shoulders twitch, as if he was trying to turn away, but then he stood still, only his head moving in time with the long, slow sway of the chain. Soon, the Baron slackened and slumped, just as Lotus Blossom had done.

'The Magi said to him, "You will do as I tell you and when we are finished and I snap my fingers, you will forget everything that has happened." His voice was slow and smooth, his words keeping time with the rhythm of the chain. Just watching them, I felt a weariness steal over me, as if I was sinking underwater.

'But at his next command, I nearly fell off my bench.

'"You will go to your bedchamber," the Magi told him, "and collect all your gold and jewels and the titles to your lands and properties and put them in this big wooden chest here. Then you will carry the chest to the bottom of your garden and hide it in your underground storeroom by the river. You will come back and go to bed and you will sleep soundly until I snap my fingers in the morning."

'I leapt up, pinching my cheeks to wake myself up, and crept silently after the Baron. And he did exactly as he had been told to do. He staggered down to the jetty with the heavy chest and put it on the table in the underground storeroom. The Magi followed him back to the house, and I followed the Magi.

'I waited until I saw a light go out in the Baron's bedroom, and then I walked home. What to do? My mind still felt oddly underwater. I took my time, feeling the fresh night air on my skin, stopping to watch the starlight glinting through the trees. I had a lot to think about.

'The next morning there was a great uproar. The Baron was charging through the village bellowing that he had been robbed. "All my jewels and gold and precious papers are gone!" he roared. "Who has done this to me? I'll find the thief, I'll tear him apart! How dare you!"

'He was glaring at the shopkeepers, who ran out of their doors to see what all the noise and fury was about. If the Baron had been a dragon, smoke would have been billowing out of his nose! He barged into Not Yet's shoemaking shop, and picked up a waiting boy by his collar. Shaking him, he didn't let go until the boy's father came running in to save him. "It couldn't have been *my* son!" he cried. "He was helping me all night with our sick cow. Why don't you look to that stranger in town – the Magi – instead of one of your honest tenants!"

'The Baron dropped the boy like a burning coal without even so much as a "sorry", swinging away on his heel. We heard later that he bailed up the Magi, who insisted that he was innocent and must be searched – and of course, nothing was found.

'Something had to be done, quickly. I called on Lotus Blossom and Ah Chu and told them the whole story. They couldn't believe me at first. "Come on," I said. "I'll show you."

'We carefully made our way through the Baron's gardens, down into the underground storeroom. The cold stone walls were damp with green slime, and moss grew at the back where water seeped in from the river. Ah Chu shivered. In the gloom, they saw the wooden chest was still there on the table, the lid open to reveal a small mountain of gleaming jewels. We peeped in, and gazed in wonder. There were ruby rings and emerald earrings, strings of pearls and necklaces of silver. Lotus Blossom stretched out her hand for a moment. It was so hard not to touch the little gold brooches of bees, dragons, birds, and serpents that looked like spell-bound animals in an enchanted forest.

'"What do you think we should do?" asked Ah Chu.

"'I'm trying to decide," I said. I had to look away from the jewels so I could think. "On the one hand most of the gold was probably stolen by the Baron. On the other hand the Magi is certainly a very bad man and should be stopped. On the other hand—"

"'You've already used two hands," Ah Chu pointed out.

"'On the other hand," a silky voice slid into the conversation, "it might not be a very good idea to make an enemy of the Magi."

'We froze. There he was, calmly leaning against the doorpost at the top of the stairs that led down to the storeroom. We stood, gaping up at him.

"'We won't tell anyone," croaked Ah Chu. "We were just going."

"'No, I don't think I can allow you to do that," the Magi crooned.

'Two ropes were hanging inside the doorway. The Magi thoughtfully pulled on one of them. A small wooden door was set into the wall behind us. It slid up, exposing an iron grille with bars like a prison cell. Behind the grille, a huge alligator stared out at us. Its long mouth was filled with enormous pointed teeth.

Two ropes were hanging inside the doorway.

We yelped in fright and it snapped at us, its mouth yawning wide enough to swallow us whole.

'The Magi laughed, and his hand moved towards the second rope to pull up the grille.

'I had to stop him. "If you let that alligator out, how are you going to come down here and get that chest?"

'That took the smile off his face, I can tell you.

'"Yes, you didn't think of that, did you?" crowed Lotus Blossom. "Not so magnificent *now*, are you Magi? You great big alligatoring bully!"

'I frowned at Lotus Blossom, not wanting her to incite the Magi to some new wickedness. But his eyes had focused on hers, and he was getting something out of his waistcoat. *Oh, please, not the medal,* I thought. But just then heavy footsteps sounded, hurrying down the path towards us.

'The Baron loomed up behind the Magi. "What are you all doing down here in my secret storeroom?" bellowed his familiar voice. His eyes bulged. "And what is my missing chest doing down here?"

'The Magi smiled quickly. "I was just coming to get you, my dear Baron. These children broke into your

17

house last night and robbed you. They hid the chest
down here, intending to come back and fetch it later.
We have caught them red-handed."

"'No we didn't!" Ah Chu cried.

"'He's lying!" Lotus Blossom shouted.

'But I had been inspecting the Baron closely. "How
did you get that green slime on the sleeve of your coat
and the side of your boot if *you* didn't come down here
yourself, Baron?"

"'What?! Do you think I robbed myself?"

"'No, but last night, through your library window,
I saw the Magi hypnotise you. He made you fill that
chest with your treasures and gold and carry it here.
You put it on this table."

'The Baron looked carefully at his boot and sleeve,
comparing it with the slime on the walls of the storeroom.
He turned furiously on the Magi, who went as white
as an onion. "I...I...arrgh!" he spluttered as the Baron
pushed him down the steps and jumped on him. He
was calling for his men to come and take the Magi away
when we slipped past them and out into the warm fresh
breeze.'

'Did the Baron give you a reward for saving his fortune?' Jack asked.

'No, of course not,' said Tashi. 'Instead, he expected *us* to thank him for saving us from the alligator!'

'What was the alligator doing down there, anyway?' asked Angus.

Tashi rolled his eyes. 'The Baron said he'd bought it from the River Pirate and was going to sell it to the zoo in the city. Who knows, it might even be true.'

'I've seen an alligator,' said Angus. 'They look pretty much like our crocodiles.'

'My Uncle Joe once wrestled a big old saltwater croc with his bare hands,' said Jack. 'Then he killed it and ate it.'

'That's impossible,' said Angus.

'Is not,' said Jack. He got his wallet out of his back pocket. 'Hey Angus?'

'Yeah?'

'Ask me for five dollars.'

TASHI AND THE
BURNING HOUSE

'SCHOOL HOLIDAYS ARE coming up soon, aren't they?' said Dad. He was sorting through the laundry basket, looking for a shirt to iron. 'I was thinking we might all go away somewhere this year.'

'Oh?' said Mum. 'That doesn't sound like you. Have you got a temperature?'

Dad put down his shirt and felt his forehead. 'No, I don't think so. I just feel like an adventure. What about you, Jack?'

'Well,' said Jack. 'It depends what *kind* of adventure. Like, where would we go?'

'I don't know, somewhere different, out in the wild,' said Dad. 'I want to go camping and not have to wear ironed shirts, and catch trout while I'm watching dolphins surf. I may even ride on a dolphin's back!'

'I wonder what a dolphin feels like?' said Mum.

'Pretty happy, I'd say,' said Dad. 'They're always smiling. Probably because they don't have to wear ironed shirts.'

'For a start,' said Jack, 'dolphins live in the sea and trout live in fresh water. You can't have both *together*.' He rolled his eyes. 'You know, sometimes an adventure comes to you, rather than you going to find it.' He started to hum a little tune.

'Aha, I know that tune!' cried Dad. 'That's your *I-know-a-Tashi-story-you-don't-know* tune.'

Jack laughed.

Dad did a little skip as he went to plug in the iron. 'What is it this time? Wicked warlords, gluey ghosts, that greedy old Baron?'

'Don't you have to get to work?' said Mum.

'Oh, there's always time for a story,' said Dad airily. 'I can iron while I listen. I can multi-fast like anyone else.'

21

'That's multi-*task*,' said Jack, 'which means you can do lots of things at once.' He looked doubtful.

But Dad was sure. 'Plenty of time. And look, Mum's got your eggs ready.' His eyebrows twitched with excitement.

'Well,' said Jack, sitting down at the table, 'it was like this. Back in Tashi's old country, the school holidays were coming up.'

'Oh that's a marvellous feeling, I remember that!' Dad cut in. 'You wake up and at first you think, gosh I'm late, where's my school shirt, did I do my maths homework and then you remember, oh, it's—'

'Yes,' said Jack. 'Tashi woke up with just that happy holiday feeling. He got up and ran out of the house—'

'What, without his breakfast?'

'Oh Dad, I don't know, he didn't *tell* us that. All I know is he ran over to Lotus Blossom's house. He wanted to start the holidays straight away.

'"Come in," she called when he knocked on the door.

'"I thought we might go into the forest today," said Tashi. "We could build a cubby house..."

'But she shook her head. "Sorry Tashi, I can't.

I've promised to go and hear Mi Tu practise his new song."

'Tashi stood there for a moment, waiting for her to say, "Why don't you come too?" but she didn't, so he nodded and walked back to the gate. Some of the good feeling had dribbled away.

'And when Tashi got to Ah Chu's house, he was packing a bag of snacks. Tashi called through the window, "I thought we might go into the forest today, but it looks as if you already have something to do?"

'"That's right," said Ah Chu. "Lotus Blossom and I are meeting Mi Tu at his uncle's house." Tashi waited for Ah Chu to say "Why don't you come with us?" but he didn't, and Tashi walked on feeling quite—'

'Left out?' said Mum.

'*Sad*,' said Dad sadly.

'So what was going on?' asked Mum.

'Well, ever since Mi Tu had arrived back in the village, he had been the centre of attention. He was the son of Teacher Pang's Younger Brother, but his parents had been killed in a landslide not long ago.

'Of course everyone felt very sorry for him but that

wasn't the only reason for the interest people were taking in him. Mi Tu had the most beautiful voice anyone had ever heard; clear and pure and rich. When he sang happy songs people couldn't keep still, they had to jump up to dance and clap their hands. When his songs were sad, hankies were passed around as eyes filled and overflowed. But that wasn't all.

'Word had got about that Mi Tu owed his thrilling voice to a potion that had been a secret in his family for years and years. His father had given him the recipe before he died. Just a sip of the magical stuff each morning was all he needed to sound like a nightingale for the rest of the day!'

Dad gasped. 'Was it really a magic potion?'

'Well, that's what Tashi wanted to know. One day near the end of term, he'd seen Ah Chu walking home with Mi Tu. They were walking very slowly, their heads bent together. Later, when Tashi asked what they'd been talking about, Ah Chu's face lit up. "Guess what? Mi Tu said that one day he might just give his best friends a *taste* of his famous recipe." Ah Chu's eyes shone. "Imagine, Tashi, being able to sing so everyone wanted to listen, so everyone crowded round to hear you." And he'd stood quiet and still, gazing at this picture in his imagination.

'But Tashi didn't stay quiet. Instead he said, "I agree that Mi Tu has a wonderful voice, but I'm suspicious about this secret mixture."

'"Well, you shouldn't be!" Ah Chu burst out. "And anyway, in the meantime, Mi Tu said that for a small price, he might give us singing lessons."

'This time Tashi said nothing. But deep inside he wondered if singing lessons would make much difference to someone like Ah Chu, who had a voice like a sick frog.

'Tashi had tried to talk about his suspicions with Lotus Blossom, but she'd looked at him reproachfully. "Yes, I know, but it doesn't matter if there's a magic potion or not, does it, Tashi? For one thing it makes us so happy to hear his songs. Are you sure you're not a little bit jealous?"

'Tashi thought about this. He wasn't sure, which made him feel worse. And now, here was the first day of the holiday, a day he and Lotus Blossom and Ah Chu always spent together, and they were going off without him.

'Well, he would just take Pongo for a walk, and see
what Hai Ping was doing instead. Lotus Blossom and
Ah Chu weren't the only berries on the bush!

'The next few days Tashi spent happily with the other
children from the village, but one afternoon he just felt
like pottering about alone. As he walked along the path
leading out of the village, he started thinking of the
Haunted House and how he and his friends had saved
Ning Jing from her horrible cousin there. He wondered
if it was still standing and he decided to go and see.

'The house looked just the same, gloomy and
forbidding, overhung by trees. He stood for a few
moments in a pool of shade, remembering. Wind rustled
through the branches, tapping at a cracked window. He
crept near, curious, goosebumps rising on his skin. And
then he heard voices coming from inside. One voice
stood out from the others.

'He knew those thrilling tones!

'Sure enough, when he peered through the glass,
he saw Lotus Blossom and Ah Chu sitting spellbound.
Mi Tu was singing the haunting song of a lonely
mermaid. Tashi began to feel tearful himself, and he

couldn't help letting out a little moan. Lotus Blossom jerked out of her trance, her head turning to the window. Quickly, Tashi inched out of view – he didn't want to talk to anyone right now. He leaned against the wall, hot and uncomfortable. But then he noticed Mi Tu had stopped singing.

"'Oh why are you stopping?" cried Lotus Blossom. "That was so beautiful."

"'Really?" Mi Tu's voice sounded offended. "You were looking out the window. I thought you were bored."

'Ah Chu and Lotus Blossom began protesting, trying to outdo each other with praise… "Your singing is like a nightingale's"…"you're not from this world"…"there's no voice like yours!" And yet for all these admiring cries, Mi Tu still didn't sing a note.

'Tashi crept back and peeped through the window. He saw a strange thing. Mi Tu was searching the friends' faces hungrily. He was drinking in their words, only there didn't seem to be enough of them. He needed *more*.

'Ah Chu and Lotus Blossom's cries dried up into silence. They shifted uneasily on the floor. Just then, Mi Tu gave a little false laugh, and leapt up. "I know!"

he crowed. He danced over to the mantelpiece near the mirror and grabbed the bundle of candles lying there. "I can do magic too!"

'Chanting softly, he placed ten candles at equal distance from each other in a circle around Ah Chu and Lotus Blossom. His words were not like any Tashi knew. But as Mi Tu took a box of matches from his pocket and lit the candles, the words changed and he was singing the sweetest song Tashi had ever heard. It was like the wind behind the trees, the current in a river – somehow it moved everything inside you.

'Tashi listened and daydreamed. He watched the candlelight flare in the dim room, and a lick of horror began to rise in his stomach. He didn't want to wake from the dream-song, but he couldn't stop his eyes roaming the room...the rotting wooden boards, the drift of dry leaves on the floor, the sticks blown in by the wind. *Wah!* The house was a tinderbox. It was so dangerous!

'Without meaning to, he yelped in alarm. Lotus Blossom looked up and this time she saw him through the window. "Tashi!" she called. "Come and hear this! Mi Tu knows so many beautiful songs."

'She sprang up to open the door. But as she took her
first step, her heel flicked a candle, and knocked it over.
The flame caught, and flew along the floor. It was like
a lightning strike – it happened so quickly. A heap of
leaves in the corner sparked into life. With a loud
crackle, the fire spread out, feeding on the dry-as-dust
timber like a match to kindling. In a roar, the fire raced
up the wall.

'"Quick, use your coat!" cried Ah Chu, pulling off his
jacket and beating at the flames. He and Mi Tu leapt
about, shouting, trying to stamp out the fire. But they
were losing valuable time.

'Lotus Blossom tugged at the heavy door. "I can't open
it!" she screamed.

'"Step back now," called Tashi from outside. "I'll open
it from here!" But the door was swollen and stuck tight.

'Smoke was clouding the room and the heat was
crushing. Ah Chu stumbled over to help pull the door
open, but it was jammed shut. He ran to the window,
covered his elbow with his jacket, and smashed it against
the glass. The window shattered instantly. "Come on,
we'll climb out through here!" he called.

'Mi Tu was right behind him and it wasn't until they were standing outside with Tashi that they realised Lotus Blossom wasn't with them.

'Icy dread dropped into Tashi's stomach. He peered in through the wall of flames. "There, there!" cried Ah Chu next to him, pointing to a Lotus-Blossom-shape lying by the door.

'"We have to get her out," said Tashi. He was thinking fast. Water, he needed something wet to shield them from the heat. "Give me your jacket!" he told Ah Chu. He whipped off his own and ran to the old well in the courtyard. The well hadn't been used for years, but when he lowered its bucket, he heard a splash as it hit the bottom. He pulled it up. Good. It was full. He plunged the coats into the muddy water.

'"I'll come in with you," said Ah Chu when he got back with the dripping jackets.

'"And I'll run for help," said Mi Tu. His face was white.

'"You'll be too late," cried Ah Chu, but Mi Tu was already off and away along the darkening path.

'It was just as well Tashi and Ah Chu were wrapped in their sopping coats, but even so they could hardly bear the heat and smoke and terror of the inferno roaring around them.

'They wrapped Ah Chu's wet shirt around Lotus Blossom and picked her up by the shoulders and legs. But now the whole room was a raging furnace. They saw it was impossible to get back to the window through the flames.

'"Upstairs!" Tashi called. "It hasn't taken hold up there yet."

'"But how will we get down again?" Ah Chu yelled above the bellow of fire.

'Tashi didn't answer. He was thinking furiously.

'They dragged Lotus Blossom up the rickety stairs and across the landing. Tashi ran into a bedroom and grabbed some bedcovers off a bed. Then he pulled down the curtains. "Help me knot the corners of these together," he told Ah Chu.

'They worked fast with the heavy material, panting and trying not to take deep breaths. The air was thick with grit, tasting like charcoal in their mouths. When they had made a long bulky rope, Tashi tied one end to the leg of the bed and threw the other end out the window.

'Lotus Blossom opened her eyes. "Where are we?"

"'Upstairs in a burning house and we're going to climb down these curtains to safety," Tashi told her. "You woke up just in time." He tried to sound confident, and gave her the sign of the dragon for luck.

"'I don't think I can do it," croaked Lotus Blossom. "I can hardly breathe."

"'We'll help you," said Tashi. "Ah Chu will go first and then you can follow. If you fall, you'll have something nice and soft to land on."

'Ah Chu snorted, but just then they heard a whooshing roar like an engine starting up and they looked around to see flames racing up the landing. In seconds, a towering wall of fire blocked their exit below.

"'Let's go!" shouted Ah Chu, and he scrambled out the window.

'Lotus Blossom followed and if her feet rested on Ah Chu's shoulders more often than he liked, he didn't complain.

'A few moments later they were staggering over the grass. "Keep going, *run!*" yelled Tashi, feeling the heat blasting behind him. But Ah Chu had stopped and now

...the house exploded into a huge fireball...

they all couldn't help turning to watch as the house exploded into a huge fireball, burning itself to pieces before them.

"'We're still too close!" Tashi called suddenly. "Ah Chu come ba–" Before he could finish his warning, there was a bang and a large piece of flaming roof rose in the air and then slowly descended, falling, falling...

'Ah Chu seemed glued to the ground. Lotus Blossom screamed. She tore across the grass and with all her strength pushed him aside, just as the falling timbers crashed to the very spot where he'd been standing.

'Tashi was there at once, pulling and rolling them away to safety. They knelt, panting, grinning at each other in wonder and relief.

"'Thanks, Lotus Blossom," Ah Chu growled. "It's possible that you might just have saved my life."

"'Well, it was only fair," smiled Lotus Blossom, "seeing you did come and get me out of the burning house. I'd say we were even."

'At that moment, they heard the village bus come rumbling along the forest track. Can Du, Teacher Pang and Mi Tu jumped out almost before it stopped. Looking at the blackened mess of the house and smouldering flames, they couldn't believe the friends had escaped with only a few burns and blisters.

"'It's good to be lucky in your bad luck," said Teacher Pang.

'Mi Tu shook his head, but said nothing. He was very quiet on the way back. He sat with his head lowered, not joining in the excited chatter of the other children. When Can Du asked him for a song to celebrate their escape, he bit his lip.

'Tashi leaned over and said, softly, "We're really glad we don't have to walk all the way home with these bruises and burns. It's good you went for the bus, Mi Tu, that was the right choice. It wasn't just luck that helped us."

'Mi Tu jerked his head up at Tashi, and smiled. "You are right, Tashi. It wasn't luck, it was friendship. You have good brave friends."

"'And now we have another," said Tashi, "with you. Maybe we *are* lucky!"

'And they sang an escape-from-the-burning-house song all the way home.'

'How did that tune go?' said Dad. 'I wouldn't mind hearing it.'

Jack laughed. 'Tashi will have to come over and sing it. But of course he can't sing it like Mi Tu.'

'So there wasn't really any magic mixture?' said Dad.

'No. Mi Tu just had an amazing gift. He thought he had to make himself extra special with that story, but he learned to believe in his voice, and in his friends. Tashi said he gave great singing lessons, but Ah Chu never really learned to sing in tune – he wasn't very disappointed though because he got interested in something else. He found a great fishing spot near the Dragon's Blood Tree, and Big Wu showed him some of his famous recipes. Everyone wanted to come over to eat his fish and tell stories and listen to Mi Tu's songs.'

Dad sighed. 'Ah! *That's* the way to live… So how about *we* go somewhere these holidays and discover a great fishing spot? What do you say?'

'Can Tashi come?'

'Will the sun rise tomorrow?' said Mum and Dad together.

Tashi and the
Orchid Thieves

'That's the best fish I've ever tasted,' said Dad.

'Mmm,' said Mum, looking across the camp fire at
Jack and Tashi. 'But watch out for bones, won't you.'

The boys nodded. Firelight danced across their faces,
greasy with fish and salad. Behind them the bush was
dark. In front, only a stone's throw away, was the river.

'Can we swap fishing rods tomorrow, Tashi?' asked
Jack.

'Sure,' said Tashi, who'd caught all the trout they'd had
for dinner. 'And I'll show you how I cast my line.'

'Me too,' sighed Dad. 'Maybe then I'll catch something.'

'I want to find more wildflowers,' said Mum, lying back and looking up at the stars. 'Like those creamy ones I saw today. The petals were as soft as my good cashmere cardigan–'

'Flannel flowers,' said Jack.

'Yes, I know,' said Mum. 'And those beautiful yellow and white flowers–'

'Native orchids,' said Jack. 'But remember, you're not allowed to pick them. They're *wild* flowers. And very special.'

'I know, but surely we could take home just one.'

'If everybody picked one,' Jack pointed out, 'there wouldn't be any to see in the wild.'

In the quiet they heard Mum sigh. The cicadas throbbed in the velvety dark and the sky went on forever, alight with stars.

'Once, back in the old country, I found a very special orchid in the forest,' Tashi whispered into the stillness. 'It was worth a lot of money.'

Mum sat up. 'Did you pick it?'

'Of course he didn't!' crowed Dad. 'But I bet somebody else tried to, hey? Who was it? I bet I know–'

'Oh Dad,' said Jack, 'let him tell it *his* way. You can't start a story right from the end!'

'No, no,' agreed Dad hastily. 'Sorry Tashi, let's hear it… and what could be a better place than round a camp fire? Just like the days of old. So, how does it start?'

'Well,' said Tashi, 'it was like this. There was a time when the village was buzzing with gossip and rumours. People were passing on the word that a certain person was back.'

'Who?' asked Dad.

Jack held up a warning hand.

'Everywhere you went there were whispers – in Not Yet's shop when you dropped off your shoes, at Wise-as-an-Owl's house when you waited for medicine, in the village square, at the post office – everyone was talking about him.' Tashi stared into the fire. A bird called out like a whip snapping.

Dad jumped. 'So what was his name, this certain person?'

'They called him Stoneface.' Tashi picked up a stick and threw it onto the fire. 'He was a man who'd grown up in the village. When he was young his family was kidnapped by soldiers, but he was the only one who managed to escape. He made his way back to the village, and even though many families invited him to stay, he lived mostly by himself. The villagers stopped pestering him after a while, because he grew into a surly young man with a menacing manner. There was nothing they could do. He'd hit you as soon as look at you. And then one night, after a terrible fight in a tavern, he disappeared.'

'Maybe he went looking for his family?' suggested Dad.

'Maybe,' said Tashi. 'But most people believed the story that he'd joined a band of robbers, become their leader even – then ended up in gaol.

'Now he was back, and everyone was suspicious. What was he doing there? Did he still see the other members of his gang? Would they be joining him in the village?'

Mum clicked her tongue. 'Why would you return to a place where so much had gone wrong?'

'Well,' said Tashi, 'he didn't actually return to his family home – it was in ruins. Someone reported that he'd moved into a woodcutter's old shack deep in the forest. Then he started coming into the village for supplies. He said nothing, just strode across the square with a face as blank as stone. No feeling passed across it, no light flickered in his eyes. The shopkeepers were frightened of him. They decided not to sell him anything, hoping to starve him out.

'But Not Yet took pity on him. He remembered him as a very young boy, before his family was stolen, and he gave him some work to do in the shop in exchange for food.'

'I always liked Not Yet,' put in Dad. 'Never one to judge people hastily. Or point the finger.'

'Yes,' said Tashi. 'And it was at his shop that I first met Stoneface. He was serving Granny White Eyes–'

'Oh, I remember her!' said Jack. 'The blind woman who helped you find your way through the fog back to the village.'

'That's right,' nodded Tashi. 'And now she was having trouble finding the shoes she'd left to be heeled. People were waiting in the queue behind her, and Granny was getting flustered. But Stoneface just gently asked her to describe them, placing pair after pair into her hands to feel. She was calmed by his patient voice, and she soon found the right ones. I was next, and because I liked the way he'd talked to Granny White Eyes, I gave him a big smile. "It's a pleasure to meet you!" I told him.

'After that, we became friends. Stoneface told me how he regretted the life he'd led and how he wished he could undo the bad things that had happened. "I wanted to save my family," he said. "I always thought I would find a way to rescue them, but they just vanished. I was angry with the world for that, angry with myself. Now I want to do better."

'We talked about a lot of things when we went fishing in the river, or collecting firewood in the forest. And he taught me some useful tackling throws – for defence, he said sternly – and how to give a series of piercing whistles if ever I should need help.'

Tashi stopped suddenly and put two fingers on his lower lip. He curled his tongue between his teeth, and blew. The first shrill note was as loud as a siren.

Mum and Dad squealed with surprise.

It was followed by a short high-pitched whip, ending with a long note the same as the first. *WHeeeeee – whip – WHeeeeee!*

'Like that,' said Tashi.

'Do it *again*,' said Jack.

'No!' cried Mum and Dad, but it was too late.

'I reckon that whistle would stop a lion charging,' shuddered Dad, taking his fingers out of his ears.

'Sorry,' said Tashi, making a face.

'Go on,' laughed Mum. 'Just warn us next time.'

'Well,' said Tashi, 'Stoneface also told me some thrilling stories about the lawless big city. When Lotus Blossom and Ah Chu heard about them, they wanted to meet Stoneface too. I wasn't sure how they'd all like each other, but in the end I agreed to take them into the forest to see him.

'We tramped through the thick bush, and we'd nearly reached his shack when we were startled by a loud bird call.'

'It's okay,' said Dad quickly. 'You don't have to show us – we can imagine.'

Tashi grinned. 'When I looked up, I saw a most beautiful orchid hanging high in a fig tree. Its snow-white petals were covered with glistening red spots. I thought it was the most magnificent thing I'd ever seen. As we drew nearer to it, we breathed in its perfume – a wonderful mixture of vanilla and cinnamon.

'"That's amazing!" I said to my friends. "That flower is so far up but its smell can still reach us."

'"Yes," said Ah Chu, sniffing hungrily. "It's making my mouth water."

'"That's the sweet vanilla," I said.

'"Everything makes his mouth water," laughed Lotus Blossom.

'"I've got to take a closer look," I told them, and began to climb the tree. I was quite high up, reaching for the branch above me when I heard a loud hiss. *Wah!*

'Lotus Blossom and Ah Chu called out to me but I was already falling. Frantically, I grabbed at some branches as they whipped past but caught none and I landed, luckily, on a thick bed of leaves.

'"I thought I was reaching for the next branch," I told them when I got my breath back, "but instead it was a sleeping viper!"

'Ah Chu shook his head. "Ugh! Snakes give me nightmares." But after he and Lotus Blossom had checked over my arms and legs, he said, "I wonder what that flower would smell like, up close? Why don't we wait for the snake to go, and then climb up and pick it?"

'"No," I shook my head. "Look, it's the only one
on the tree. I don't think you're supposed to touch rare
orchids growing in the wild. Let's go and ask Favourite
Aunt, she knows all about plants and she's painted lots
of orchids."

'Li Tam, my Favourite Aunt, was very excited when
I described the orchid. She searched through her books
and said, "I think I've found it! If it *is* your orchid, it's
very rare. I think this might be an important discovery.
Can you take me to see it?"

'She dug out her old box camera to take a photo of it,
but then she had a better idea. On the way back to the
forest she suggested we stop at the Post Office to ring a
Professor of Botany she had once met at the University
in the city.

'When she put me on the phone to describe the
orchid, the Professor sounded just as excited as Favourite
Aunt. He said he wouldn't wait for the photograph, he
was coming down to see it at once. I was so fired up after
the phone call that I didn't stop to check out the two
strangers who were lounging nearby. A quick glance told
me they were leaning too close, as if trying to catch every

word, and I didn't like the suspicious way their eyes slid all over us. But Favourite Aunt was telling me about the famous Professor and his orchids, and I…well, I got swept away. It was only later that I realised the awful consequences. Oh, how I was to regret my carelessness!

'Professor Mah arrived the next day and we set off at once, the Professor often stopping to examine some curious plant. "This forest is a treasure house of medicines!" he exclaimed. He would get out his magnifying glass and hold it up to the leaves so we could see their veins running in complicated patterns. He explained how the leaves were the kitchens of the plants, making food from sunlight. Lotus Blossom gasped in wonder. I nodded and smiled because hadn't Wise-as-an-Owl been teaching me that very thing for years?

'In this way we took quite some time to reach the tree. But instead of looking up to see the beautiful flower amongst the leaves, a terrible sight met our eyes. The two brutish strangers I'd seen at the Post Office were standing beside the tree – with the poor plucked plant in their hands! They were pulling at the long dangling roots, trying to straighten them out.

'"Stop!" cried Professor Mah. "Unless I am mistaken, that is a rare and valuable species of orchid that has not been seen for fifty years."

'"All the better," growled one of the ruffians.

'The men laughed, and they laughed even louder when the Professor told them he would hurry back to the village and report them if they didn't give him the orchid at once. He was still scolding them when a third villain quietly came out of the trees behind him.

'This man was huge, and in his hands was a thick rope that he dropped over the Professor's head and shoulders. The Professor's eyes bulged with shock as his arms were pinned to his sides. He tried to twist and turn but the villain held the rope tight, with no effort at all. The other two men sniggered as they watched. Then they brought out knives from their belts and quick as vipers they darted, grabbing us and dragging us over to a circle of trees that grew close together.

'One of the men, who they called One Ear, began tying Favourite Aunt and me to either side of a tree. The other man pulled the struggling Lotus Blossom and

Ah Chu over to the oak next to it, binding them up with great hairy hands that scuttled everywhere at once.

"'Get off, you hairy spider!" yelled Lotus Blossom, and kicked at Hairy's ankle.

"'Ow!" he cried, enraged.

"'Ssh!" I hissed at her from my tree. "You'll only make it worse."

"'If I'm a spider, you're the fly," the hairy man spat at Lotus Blossom, "and I'm going to truss you up in my web!"

'One Ear snorted at that. Or maybe he was grunting. He seemed to be having a lot of trouble tying me up. He wasn't very good at knots. "Couldn't we just knock them on the head?" he said.

"'Or drop them in that pool of leeches over there?" Hairy suggested, scowling at Lotus Blossom.

'I heard Favourite Aunt moan from the other side of the tree.

"'No need," the huge villain stepped forward. He was the leader, I could tell, and his voice was low and sinister. "Even if the snakes don't find them, no one will hear their cries out here. Plenty of time for us to get back to the

"Get off, you hairy spider!" yelled Lotus Blossom

village and hand the orchid over to–" he glanced around, "to our friend."

'He bent to examine the clumsy knot One Ear had tied around my wrists and thighs, and clicked his teeth in disgust. Taking a new piece of rope, he bound it tightly around my chest. "Let's go," he barked, turning on his heel. He strode out through the bushes, with Hairy and One Ear crashing behind him.

'Oh, the hours ticked past so slowly! The silence was almost complete. I couldn't help thinking how much worse it would be when night fell. At every rustle in the grass, we stiffened with fear. Once, a bird shrieked in alarm, making our hearts pound.

'"I wish I knew where that viper had gone," whispered Favourite Aunt.

'The Professor gave her a gentle smile. "We mustn't give up," he said. "Someone could come by any minute."

'"I wouldn't mind so much if I wasn't so hungry," sniffed Ah Chu.

'"We're all hungry," snapped Lotus Blossom. "And Tashi, I wouldn't be surprised if that Stoneface person hadn't brought those robbers to our village, either."

'A light switched on in my head. "Of course!" I cried. "Stoneface! His shack isn't far from here. Why didn't I think of that before?"

'Lotus Blossom blinked. "What good is that? Like I just said, he's probably one of the robbers."

'"No, I'm sure he's not," I said. "We'll soon find out," and I went to raise my hands to my lips. But I'd forgotten. My wrists were tied to my thighs, bound tight to the tree. I couldn't move them.

'I ground my teeth. What was the good of knowing how to do that special whistle when your hands were tied? I looked down at the ground in despair, and that was when I saw it. A brown-gold streak in the grass.

'"*Wah!*" I couldn't help moaning. A pit viper! I saw it clearly now, sunlight gleaming on its scales. Silently, it slid towards Ah Chu's feet.

'"What?" said Lotus Blossom.

'"Oh, it's just – a bit hard to breathe under this tight rope." I glanced at Ah Chu. He was pale and sweaty, but he hadn't seen the snake. Should I warn him not to make any sudden movement with his foot? But what if he panicked, and lashed out? Oh, what to do?

'I was starting to panic now, too. *Stop struggling,* I told myself. *Empty your mind of thoughts.* I closed my eyes and waited until everything became very still. And then a memory dropped into my mind, like a stone into a clear pool.

'Wise-as-an-Owl once told me that if you happen to get tied up, you must search for even the tiniest bit of slack – the space between you and the rope. "You can always get yourself out," he said. "The trick is to find that space and keep working at it. You must never give up." But I wondered, looking at the fearful shape in the grass, if there would be the time.

'I began making small twisting movements from right to left with my shoulders, like turning a key in a lock. The rope chafed my skin. I tried to ignore the burn, focusing only on my little swivelling motions. After about fifty turns as far as I could go each way, the rope loosened slightly. Next, I found I could wriggle my wrists – One Ear really hadn't been good at his job. Hope gave me a rush of strength and I took short shallow breaths.

'"What are you doing? Why are you panting?" Lotus Blossom's voice was anxious.

'"It's…all right," I managed. And then, quite suddenly, there was enough space between the rope and my arms to slide my hands up my legs to my waist, and out, free!

'"*Snake!*" Ah Chu called out wildly. "Near me!"

'"Ssh, I know, but no need to worry if you don't move your foot," I gasped.

'Then I took a really deep breath and blew it hard through my fingers, giving three piercing whistles.

'We waited. Nothing. I whistled again. Ah Chu was trembling, but he stayed still. And then faintly, so faintly I wasn't sure if I'd heard it, there was an answering whistle.

'I signalled once more. This time the answer was much closer. Now Stoneface and I signalled backwards and forwards until finally there was the sound of breaking branches and crunching footsteps, and Stoneface burst through the trees.

'"Are you all right? Who did this to you?" he cried, running up to us.

'"Look out for the viper! There, near his feet!"
I pointed to Ah Chu.

'Stoneface threw his satchel with a thud, right near the

snake. It slithered away in fright, into the trees. He pulled out his knife and I heard Favourite Aunt gasp. Quickly he cut through the ropes, cursing as we described the evil doings of those villains.

'"What did they look like?" he asked grimly.

'When I described the men, Stoneface knew exactly who they were: the three meanest and most dangerous members of his old band of robbers. And what's more, he knew where they would be taking the orchid.

'As we charged through the forest, back to the village, Stoneface told us more. "It's a well-known fact amongst robbers," he explained, "that the Baron is someone who can be relied upon to get rid of stolen goods – for a fee, of course."

'"Let's hope we get to the Baron's house before they leave," fretted the Professor.

'We raced into the village, calling for help. People dashed out of their shops, and soon a group of strong men were running with us, down the road towards the bridge, and up the path to the Baron's house. He came out to see what we were all doing at his gate but before a word could be said, we spotted the robbers. They were down at his jetty, their pockets stuffed with banknotes, climbing onto a boat moored there.

'"I'll catch them!" yelled Stoneface, galloping ahead.

'We all pounded after him, with the Baron sprinting to catch up with us. Down at the water we arrived to see Stoneface seize the rope hanging off the boat, and haul it in.' Tashi grinned. 'I'll never forget the Baron's face as the robbers were reeled in, like fish on a line.'

'So you caught them!' cried Dad. 'And the precious orchid was saved!'

'Yes, it caused a big stir,' said Tashi. 'The Professor had thought it was very rare, but in fact it was better than that – it was a new species, never seen before. And guess what they called it!' Suddenly Tashi stopped, embarrassed.

'I know!' said Jack. 'They called it after you!'

Tashi gave a small smile, ducking his head. 'Yes,' he said. 'Tashi is part of its name. It's in all the books, the Professor even sent us a copy. I got a certificate, and the newspaper people came to take our photographs.'

'And what happened to the Baron?' asked Dad. 'Was he roasted slowly over a spit? Burnt in a bonfire of banknotes? Pecked to death by his peacock?'

Tashi laughed. 'Well, as you'd expect, once the thieves were caught everyone went looking for the orchid. The Baron hadn't had time to find a good hiding place for it, so they discovered it in the first place they went looking – his greenhouse. And of course he had no idea how the orchid got there. He said the robbers must have sneaked it in when he wasn't looking. As usual, he slithered out of it all.'

'Just like that snake!' exploded Dad.

'Well, at least he lost the orchid *and* his money,' Tashi pointed out. 'The orchid was taken to the Botanical Gardens in the city to be studied and the University was very pleased to receive a sudden big donation in the Baron's name.' Tashi smiled, as if he'd just put a lolly in his mouth. 'The Baron looked sick when everyone thanked him and he went stumping about the village with a face like thunder.'

'I'd have liked to see *that*,' said Dad.

'It's strange, you know,' Tashi went on, 'a few weeks later, the Professor and I found a cluster of those very same orchids growing in the forest. People came from all over the country to look at them. And naturally the Baron wanted to sell tickets!'

Tashi the Brave
Part One

JACK PUT TWO fingers to his lower lip and blew. Nothing happened. It was the twenty-sixth time that day, the last of their camping holiday.

'Never mind,' said Dad, who was in a good mood after catching three fish. 'That whistle could shorten a person's life span if they weren't prepared.'

Tashi, collecting kindling up ahead, chuckled.

Suddenly, an ear-splitting whistle tore the air.

Dad and Jack jumped. They dropped their fishing gear. 'I thought you were going to warn us before you did that!' Dad called to Tashi.

When they caught up, Tashi turned to face them.
'It wasn't me,' he said. 'Look, my hands are full of sticks.'
Jack saw that he was trembling slightly.

The three stood staring at each other in the twilight.
Shadows shivered at their feet, and a hook of moon
swung above the trees.

'Well,' said Dad quietly, 'what was…'

'*Wheeeee whea wheeeeeeee*,' the terrible whistle came
again.

The Stoneface whistle.

'That's so weird,' Jack shivered. 'How…'

'Run!' cried Dad. 'Back to camp!'

The boys lit up the path with Dad on their heels.
It wasn't until they reached the camping ground and
they'd told Mum, who was calmly setting a billy to boil
on the fire for tea, that Jack suddenly began to laugh.

'What's so funny, for heaven's sake?' asked Dad.
'I haven't had such a fright since the rat peeped out
of our garbage bin.'

'Look,' Jack pointed to a flowering gum. 'On that
branch.'

They all looked up to see a grey bird with a long
lacy tail.

'That's a fine bird,' said Dad, 'but I don't see…'

'Well, it's like this,' began Jack.

'Like this,' said the bird.

There was a shocked silence.

'What on earth…?' whispered Dad.

'Lyrebird,' said Jack. 'Remember, Tashi? We learned about them at school. They can mimic anything – chainsaws, mobile phones, electric drills, *whistles*… They do it to attract a mate.'

'The things we do for love,' said Mum.

'Or fear,' grinned Jack. 'You should have seen Dad run.'

Dad snorted. 'Anyone would have got a fright! Such an amazing invention!'

'It's not an invention, Dad, it's a *bird*. That's the whole point about how amazing it is.'

'You're right,' said Dad. 'And when you've got a very active imagination like me, you can't help inventing all kinds of wild and scary…well. A very fine thing, the imagination.'

Tashi nodded. 'And very powerful. Sometimes more powerful than we know.'

'Ooh,' said Dad. 'Is *yours* firing up?'

Tashi yawned. It was such a huge yawn and took so long to finish that Mum had poured the tea by the time Tashi could say, 'Yes, but I'll just change out of these wet things first,' and he wandered off up the track to the tent.

Later, when dinner was ready, Mum called Tashi. There was no answer. When Jack went to have a look, he found Tashi curled up in the tent, fast asleep.

Jack came back to the fire.

'Don't wake him,' said Mum. 'He was up before all of us this morning.'

'Yes,' said Jack. 'He discovered that great little fishing spot at the bend in the river.'

'Hmm,' sighed Dad. He picked up his fork, then put it back down. 'Does this mean we won't have a story though? On our last night around the camp fire?' His shoulders slumped. He gazed sadly at Jack.

'I could tell you a Tashi story,' Jack said. 'One you haven't heard.'

Dad looked up happily. 'Yes! He must have enough stories to fill a *book*, I reckon. So, what's this one about?'

Jack thought while he chewed. He listened to the crickets chirping steadily through the darkness that was

creeping in round the fire. When he'd finished listening
he said, 'Well, it was like this. Tashi was in the village
square one afternoon with his friends, when a rider came
galloping up to the main gate. Everyone watched as he
got off his horse and nailed up a notice from the Palace.
They crowded in to read it, and soon the air was buzzing
with excited whispers.'

'Oh, wasn't *that* the way to travel?' Dad said. 'You
know, I did a lot of horse-riding when I was a lad. Loved
it! You—'

'No interrupting,' said Jack.

'I was only remarking...'

'What did the notice from the Palace say?' asked Mum.

'Well, it was such exciting news,' Jack went on,
'that Tashi had to run straight home and tell his family.
"You'll never guess!" he cried, as soon as he burst into
the house. "The Emperor is going to hold a contest to
find the bravest person in the land. There will be a prize
of Great Riches for the winner. And guess what else?
They've worked out that our village is in the very centre
of the land, so the Emperor and his court are coming
here next week to judge the contest. They'll be staying

at the Baron's house." At this, Tashi's mother rolled her eyes. "And can you imagine," Tashi went on, "who is coming on ahead to make sure everything is in order? Tiki Pu!"

"'Oh *no*,' Grandma groaned to Tashi, "I thought we'd seen the last of that sneaky uncle of yours.'"

'Me too,' put in Dad.

'Well,' Jack went on, 'during the next few days, Tiki Pu arrived to make sure the Baron had repapered the best bedroom for his royal guest, and had plenty of peacocks in the garden. When Tashi stopped by to admire the peacocks spreading their splendid tail feathers, Tiki Pu suddenly emerged from behind a pear tree.

"'What are you doing here?" he barked. "Look, if you've come to invite me to dinner you're going to be disappointed. I have a very important job here, can't you see? You'll just have to go back and tell your mother I'm much too busy and grand to be visiting the family now." And he waved Tashi away, as if swatting a fly.'

Dad thumped the ground with his fist, knocking over his tea, which scalded his knee. He jiggled it in the air with fury. '*Urrgablungaberr!*' he cried.

'Yes,' said Jack. 'But as Tashi told Grandma when he got home, at least Tiku Pu will be staying with the Baron this time, and not taking over *his* bedroom.

'And now all sorts of people began drifting into the village. The Warlord, a Bandit Chief, the River Pirate and other warriors from all over the land rode in with their followers, hoping to show what great fighters they were.

'The Emperor frowned when he saw them. "Being a good warrior isn't always the same thing as being brave, you know. Still," he nodded to Tiki Pu, "let's see what they can do. It will be a good afternoon's sport, I suppose."

'Lots of ordinary folk who had carried out acts of bravery streamed in too. They came with their families and friends so that the village was soon bursting with visitors. All the spare beds were filled and a little settlement of tents was set up down by the river for the overflow.

'Pedlars arrived with cartloads of food, and entertainers flocked in, shaking up the sleepy town. Every night Tashi and his friends could hardly wait to go down to the river to see the fire-eaters and hear the music.

They swayed and swirled to the sounds of flutes, fiddles and drums. Mi Tu – you know, Tashi's friend with the wonderful voice – stood on a fruit crate, singing beautiful songs that made people dance and cry. He drew the crowds like nobody else.

'But on the third night, Tashi had a horrible nightmare. He dreamed he was back in the time when ghost monsters had drifted through the village, terrifying households, slithering over animals and villagers, sliding into people's open mouths and stealing the breath out of them.'

'Ugh!' shuddered Dad. 'I remember…the ghosts were disgusting, all thick and gooey and see-through, like egg white. And they were everywhere.'

'Yes,' said Jack. 'But Tashi had threatened the ghosts, remember? He tricked them by saying that his very good friend, the Red-Whiskered Dragon-Ghost, would gobble up the moon if they didn't leave the village alone. "You will all live in nights of total darkness," he'd told them.'

Jack's voice tolled out through the shivery firelight as he repeated Tashi's warning.

'But then he saved the village,' Dad put in quickly,

as Mum inched up closer. 'And the ghosts were very afraid and left because they didn't know there really *was* no such creature who could eat up the moon. Tashi had just made up the Red-Whiskered Dragon from his imagination.'

'That's right,' agreed Jack. 'But Tashi said that in his nightmare, the Red-Whiskered Dragon-Ghost was so real. He dreamed he was being chased by it: no matter how fast he ran, he could never get away. The Red-Whiskered monster was no ghost – he seemed like a real dragon!

'All through the day after the dream, Tashi was haunted by a feeling of dread. It was a heavy, tight feeling, like not being able to get enough air. Even when he was with friends at the schoolhouse, he thought if he turned around suddenly, he'd see the Red-Whiskered Dragon right there, just about to reach out and grab him.

'It wasn't until the day of the judging that Tashi was able to throw off the spooky feeling. On that morning, everything seemed different – sunlight poured cheerfully through the window and he bounced out of bed, eager to see his friends and hear the Emperor's decision. Who would be the bravest person in the land?

'The morning was hot and hazy, with a whiff of far-off smoke in the air. And it grew hotter still as a long line of hopeful people waited in the square to be presented to the Emperor. There was a young woman who had saved her little brother from a rampaging buffalo; a boy, armed only with a small knife, who had rescued his friend from the deadly clasp of a giant squid; a girl who'd pulled her mother feet-first from the jaws of a tiger; and many more.

'The villagers stood rapt, listening to these tales of bravery. "It was better than a play," Tashi said. But as the strangely smoky afternoon wore on, several people began murmuring. The murmur became louder until one name was heard clearly. "Ta-shi! *TA-SHI!*"

'Wise-as-an-Owl stepped forward. "Your Mightiness, we have a boy here in this very village who has proved himself brave not once but many, many times. His name is Tashi."

'"That's the one!" cried the villagers.

'"Did you know that he once rescued our children from the Warlord?" cried Mrs Wang.

'The Emperor looked stern at this, and the Warlord became very busy buckling his sword.

"'And what about the time he saved the village from Chintu the Giant?"

"'And his brother, don't forget," someone else called out.

"'And how he fought the flute player who had bewitched our children," cried Not Yet.

"'And he's such a lovely boy," said Granny White Eyes. "Do you know he once took me for a ride on his magic shoes? It was wonderful."

"'Yes, but that's not brave, Granny," Big Wu explained.

"'No, but it was kind," she insisted.

"'And let's not forget how he brought back the Magic Warning Bell when the River Pirate had stolen it." The Emperor sat up at this and glared at the River Pirate, who suddenly remembered he needed a haircut.

"'Yes," said Princess Sarashina, "and I am sure it has not slipped your mind, Honoured Father, how Tashi cleverly and bravely rescued me from the demons?"

'The Emperor nodded. "No, of course I couldn't forget that. But I was not thinking of a child winning the prize."

"'Why not?" asked the Princess. "Bravery has no limits of age."

'The Emperor pondered for a moment. "Very well. Bring Tashi forward."

'But before they could do it, the Magic Warning Bell began to ring and people looked up from each other's faces, and out across the horizon.

'"Fire!" yelled Lotus Blossom, hopping up and down, pointing to the next valley. And there came the bitter smell of burning, rolling in on clouds of yellow smoke.

'Just then, a family from the other side of the forest staggered into the square. "We've seen him, we've just *seen* him! With our own eyes! A great Red-Whiskered Dragon! He caused a fire in our valley."

'A Red-Whiskered Dragon? Tashi went white. He edged over to Wise-as-an-Owl. "I thought I had just made him up to frighten away the ghosts when they were threatening our village, remember?"

'"Well, he's real enough for us," said a man who overheard Tashi's whisper. "But his fire is not the worst thing about him—"

'"*What?*" said Lotus Blossom. "What could be worse?"

'"His appetite," replied the man. "He eats everything, anything. An hour ago he ate my house. Luckily there was no one home!"

"Fire!" yelled Lotus Blossom

'"Only the cow in the barn," the little boy turned to his father. "He ate her, too, remember. I *hate* that dragon!"

'Another family from the next valley had just joined the crowd. "I saw him gobble up the apple orchard of our neighbour," the grandfather said. "If he isn't stopped, we'll have nothing to eat."

'A shudder of fear drifted up through the crowd.

'Tashi plucked at Wise-as-an-Owl's sleeve, drawing him away from the square. "I really did think I had just made up that dragon, you know."

'"It happens sometimes, Tashi," Wise-as-an-Owl said softly. "When someone has a very powerful imagination and they see something in their minds, the thing becomes real when they say its name out loud."

'"Oh, no! But do you think I could pull it back into my mind again?"

'"Yes, but you would have to meet it face to face and look it in the eye."

'Tashi gulped. "Look into the eyes of a fire-breathing Red-Whiskered Dragon?"

'Wise-as-an-Owl clicked his tongue sympathetically.

"'But, Wise-as-an-Owl, I think I made him to be very fierce.'"

"'Even so.'"

'The Baron joined the Emperor on the podium. "Your Mightiness, our village is surrounded by forest. If the fire spreads, we could all be in danger. But more importantly, we could all be eaten!"'

'The Emperor had been looking anxious and now he seized eagerly on this suggestion. "Yes, indeed – we need a champion – someone extremely brave and strong. Do we have any volunteers?"'

'The Bandit Chief, the Warlord, the River Pirate and the warriors all suddenly grew quite deaf. There was complete silence in the village square.'

"'Anyone?" asked the Emperor a little desperately.'

'Tashi whispered to Wise-as-an-Owl, "I suppose, seeing that I am responsible for the Red-Whiskered Dragon's being here, I should…?"'

'Wise-as-an-Owl sighed and put his arm around Tashi's shoulders, as if to protect him. But at the same time, he nodded.'

'Tashi stepped forward.'

Jack stared into the fire. A branch crackled in a sudden gust of wind, sending up sparks. He stood up, and stretched. 'And now I have to go to bed.'

'*What?*' cried Dad. 'Without telling us what happened next?'

Jack yawned. 'I was up early, too, Dad.'

'Oh,' wailed Dad, 'that's *so* not fair!'

'You wouldn't want me to rush it, would you? Part Two of the story is the most exciting.'

'But we have no more camp-fire nights!' said Dad. 'I won't be able to sleep, I'll be haunted by ghosts. I'll be menaced to death by my active imagination!'

'Come on, let's put out this fire and get to bed too,' said Mum, taking Dad's hand. 'We've got a long drive tomorrow.'

Mum collected the plates while Jack told Dad to use his very active imagination to make up his *own* part two, whereupon Dad told Jack that was a good idea and he might just do that, but it was still unfair.

Jack wandered off to the tent, just like Tashi had earlier, already half-asleep. He even forgot to clean his teeth.

Part Two
Face to Face

IN THE MORNING, when they'd packed the last bag into the car, Mum jingled the keys. 'I'll drive,' she said. 'I had a good sleep.'

Dad gazed bleary-eyed around him. 'Goodbye tent, goodbye camp fire, goodbye trout fishing, goodbye peaceful river, goodbye lyrebird invention, goodbye summer…'

'And hello Part Two,' said Tashi.

Dad smiled for the first time that morning.

When they were on their way, and driving through the hills, Tashi took up the story where Jack had left it.

'Everybody was very relieved – and a bit ashamed – when I said that I would try to get rid of the Dragon. But I felt myself starting to tremble: the Red-Whiskered Dragon of my dream was still with me, and now, one way or another, I was going to face him in real life.'

Dad shook his head. 'How do you kill a nightmare? That's the hardest thing ever.'

'I had to hide my fear,' Tashi said. 'I stepped up onto the podium and announced, "I will find the dragon and do what I can, but I will need a little time to prepare a plan."

'The Emperor nodded gravely and wished me luck. As I walked down the steps and out of the village square, people called out their good wishes and advice. With each footstep their voices grew fainter and my fears grew louder; I'd never felt so lonely in my life.

'But I knew there was someone who could help me – my friend the Raven.'

'Oh yes,' Dad turned around to Tashi in the back seat. 'You did him a big favour once, when he was all weak and thirsty, and you rescued him from that fallen branch.'

'I remember!' cried Mum. 'That was my favourite story – with the Baba Yaga. Oh, dear, I just missed the turn-off.'

Mum bit her lip. 'You know, I'm going to have to ask you to wait, Tashi, until we stop for morning tea. I can't concentrate on driving when there are Ravens and Red-Whiskered Dragons in the car.'

Luckily, Dad found quite soon that he needed to go to the toilet, and there, right up ahead, was a welcoming-looking tea shop.

When they were settled comfortably at a large table, Mum ordered a big plate of raisin toast. 'So, how did you find the Raven?' Mum asked.

'It wasn't hard,' Tashi said. 'He was in the mulberry tree when I ran home, and he flew down straight away when I whistled. He listened carefully while I told him my problem.

'"What we need," I explained, "is to find out everything we can about the Dragon. Where is his cave? Is he clever or cunning, cowardly or brave? You see, I haven't ever actually seen him."

'The Raven gazed at me thoughtfully. "I will do what I can," he promised.

'I crossed my fingers for luck and went to fetch my magic running shoes. In just a few minutes I could travel across whole fields and forests in those shoes, and who knew how far away the Dragon lived?'

'Do you want jam with that?' asked the waitress, hovering nearby.

'Oh, yes please,' said Jack.

'There was only time to pull on the magic shoes and pack my bag before the Raven returned,' said Tashi. 'He told me that the Dragon was living in a cave on Crimson Mountain, across the valley. "You'll see the mountain from the river – the lower slopes are covered in a carpet of red flowers."

'"And the Dragon himself? What's he like?"

'"Well, right now he has indigestion. He is always grizzling about the local food. But the main thing about him is that he's very vain. He does nothing but sit admiring himself in a mirror, combing his whiskers and eating his way through a great mountain of apples."

'"Thank you, Raven, that's very interesting," I said, and hurried back to the village where everyone was still milling around anxiously. I found Wise-as-an-Owl, and spoke to him.

'"Listen, everyone," he called to the villagers. "Tashi has a good plan but he'll need some help."

"'Yes, yes of course," they all cried.

"'First, I'll need garlands of flowers," I told them.

"'Easily done," several people shouted, glad to have
a simple, safe task.

"'Wait a moment, I haven't finished. I will also need
four white sheets. They must be cut in halves to make eight
banners. And we'll need paint, black and red if you can
find it, so it will show up well when you write the slogans."

"'What slogans?"

"'I'm coming to that," I said. "But there is one more
important thing. Some people must come halfway up
the mountain with me and wait at a distance from the
Dragon's cave."

'Faces fell. People glanced nervously at each other.
My Mother and Father, Grandmother and Grandfather
stepped up. "Of course we'll come, Tashi."

"'And me," cried Favourite Aunt.

"'And me, and me," cried Big Wu and Not Yet.

"'We'll all come!" shouted Lotus Blossom, Ah Chu and
Granny White Eyes, and after a small pause, Luk Ahed.

'The Warlord cleared his throat. "I had best stay
behind and guard the Emperor."

'The Bandit Chief and the River Pirate thought that really, all things considered, taking into account the dangerous nature of the situation, they should stay too.

'The Baron explained that as he was the Emperor's host, he couldn't very well leave his royal guest to go off adventuring up a mountainside. The villagers grinned knowingly and turned to leave, discussing as they went who would gather the flowers and who would paint the sheets.

'But as the River Pirate hurried off, Wise-as-an-Owl appeared at his side. "We'll need you to take Tashi and his helpers up the river in your boat."

'"Oh, but I can lend it to them, no need for me to come," said the River Pirate generously. "Don't worry, I won't be using it for a few days."

'There was a long silence while Wise-as-an-Owl gazed at him meaningfully, and everyone turned to look.

'"Oh, all right," he mumbled.

'We all met up again down at the Baron's wharf. The villagers hauled sacks of flowers and big bright banners onto the boat, and the River Pirate let loose the rope. Luckily there was a strong breeze and the sail filled

out under clouds scudding across the sky. We travelled
at good speed, past the Dragon's Blood Tree and the
Warlord's castle, and through the deep valleys in between.

When we'd rounded the last bend, we saw Crimson
Mountain rise up from the forest a short distance away.
We were cheered by this, but as we drew up to a small
jetty and stepped out, the smell of burning leaves and
danger met us.

"'Best if I wait here at the river for you," the River
Pirate said quickly. "Or maybe over there," he said,
pointing to a small island at a safe distance.

'Not Yet turned to me. "What do you need from us?"

'I told them to come with me to the foot of the
mountain and wait there. Then I explained what to do
when I gave the signal.

'Loaded up with bundles, we headed off through
the forest. Not Yet had borrowed the River Pirate's
sword, and he went ahead, hacking at the vines and
bushes blocking our path. It seemed as if we were the
first people ever to enter this forest. All around were
smoldering cinders, and further off, leaping flames.
Smoke stung our eyes, making it hard to see, but soon

we were clear of the forest and on bare rocky ground. The mountain rose up sheer and sharp before us.

'There was no time to lose. "Wait here," I told them. "Sparks won't catch on the rocks, you should be safe."

'I took a running start and bounded up the mountainside in my magic shoes. I didn't take a moment to think or get my breath – I didn't want to let the fear build up inside me any more than it already had.

'I found the Dragon's cave easily enough because a mound of bones was piled outside. I stood quietly at the entrance. It was dim inside, and I had to wait for my eyes to grow used to it after the bright day at my back. A shudder rode through me and the terror of my dream rose up behind my eyes. I remembered how the Dragon monster had chased me, almost grabbing me. I remembered the lurking, suffocating doom of him. And now, here, framed in candlelight, was the mighty Red-Whiskered Dragon himself. Here was the very real proof of my imagination.

'He was lounging in a chair, legs crossed, admiring himself in a mirror, just as the Raven had said. His red whiskers curled out from his jaws in rippling waves.

'I cleared my throat. "Good afternoon, Mighty Red-Whiskered Dragon. May I come in? You may remember me. My name is Tashi."

'The Dragon sat up and narrowed his great green eyes. "Why are you here?"

'"To see you, of course," I replied. "To see if you are as magnificent as people have been saying."

'The Dragon relaxed. "And *am* I?" he smirked, looking into the mirror again.

'"Much, much more handsome," I gushed, "if only…"

'"If only what?" demanded the Dragon indignantly.

'I stepped right up to the Dragon and examined him carefully. "If only we could add a few finishing touches, here and there."

'The Dragon picked up the mirror. "What touches?"

'I walked slowly around the Dragon. "Well, these splendid scales are a bit dull. If we could just polish them up and oil that tremendous tummy, and," I added, peering up at the Dragon's red-hot mouth, "if those fearsome teeth were filed into deadly points, you would be quite perfect." I took a step back as he burped loudly. His hot breath smelled of rotting meat. "See?" I quickly pointed outside. "Already people have come from near and far, bringing you garlands to hang on your horns, but imagine if we made those little improvements... You would be hailed as the most magnificent dragon in all the world."

'The Dragon went to the cave entrance and looked down. Standing beside him, I gave the first signal and the villagers stood up and waved their garlands and held up the banners.

'I gave the second signal, and in their loudest voices, all together, the villagers cheered the slogans they were holding up:

"*Long live the Mighty Red-Whiskered Dragon.*
Hurrah for the Magnificent Firedrake.
Three Cheers for our Dazzling Dragon.
The Wonder of the World!"

'The Dragon turned back to me. "Do it," he said.

'From my pocket I brought out the magnifying glass the Professor had given me. "I have brought you this present," I said, and showed him how to use it. "You can watch how your scales and teeth start to shine."

'I took a cloth and some fragrant smelling oil out of my bag and, sitting astride the Dragon, (hiding a shiver), I rubbed the oil into his belly. While I worked, he played with the magnifying glass. He held it up to his scales, absorbed in the shining beauty of himself.

'When I'd finished with his tail, polishing until it glowed, he sprang up and pranced around the cave.

'"I'll have to get some more mirrors," he gloated, and a burst of fire streamed out of his mouth, singeing the tips of my hair. I took out some cutters and trimmed the Dragon's talons and buffed them till they shone.

'"That's better. So graceful and deadly," crowed the Dragon, waving them about.

'I took a deep breath. "And now for your teeth."

'I climbed up the Dragon's chest and pulled out my file. "Open, please."

'The Dragon lay back, quite relaxed. He dropped his jaw and contemplated the ceiling. "You know, I really should put a mirror up there. Especially if I'm going to have more of these marvellous manicures."

'"What a good idea," I replied. I nodded enthusiastically, trying to catch his eye. My heart thudded.

The giant lizard shifted his head. He was lowering his gaze, he was looking into my face...*BUMP!*

'I was tossed into the air and crashed to the ground. Had the Dragon guessed what I was trying to do? He glared at me, his green eyes glinting.

'I crouched where I had fallen, waiting.

'"You should do something about those sharp little knees of yours," he growled. "They were sticking into me. Gives me indigestion."

'"Perhaps if I climb up your tail and sit on your back where the scales are thicker?"

'"Yes, that would be better."

'I scrambled up the oily spine and looked into the mirror over the Dragon's shoulder. My moment had come – I had to deal with the monster now, face to face.

'"How red your whiskers are and how wavy your horns." We admired them together, the Dragon and I. Our eyes met in the mirror.

'The Dragon found that he couldn't look away. He struggled and squirmed, his whole body heaving. But the more he tried to escape, the more stuck he became. His eyes were caught by mine. I didn't blink. My gaze was a magnet, and he was held fast.

Our eyes met in the mirror.

'With every second that passed – whisker by whisker, scale by scale – his outline grew fainter. The green of his eyes turned milky, his talons frayed. He was becoming flimsy, almost see-through, until he shrank into a pale green smudge that drifted down, down into my left eye. The end of his tail gave a protesting twitch – and he disappeared.

'I had pulled him back into my mind.

'A shudder passed through me, and something sour spurted into my throat. I gulped and shook as my stomach twisted in a hot wave of disgust.

'I sat quietly for a time with my eyes closed. I don't know how many minutes passed before my breathing slowed. A whimper of smoke wafted in the air, stale and sad. When I could stand without wobbling, I went outside to wave "All's well".

'From down below a huge cheer burst out, and the villagers came scrambling up the mountain to meet me. They looked around the empty cave, whistled at the great pile of bones, and hoisted me up on their shoulders.

'There was much singing and exclaiming as we made our way back to the village.

"'Did you see the size of him standing there beside Tashi?"

"'He was as big as the giant Chintu!"

"'And that great burst of fire coming out of his mouth!"

"'I don't suppose you could tell us how you managed to get rid of him, Tashi?" asked Not Yet, skipping along beside me.

"It was a kind of magic," I explained, "but I don't really dare to say any more about it in case talking about it undoes the magic."

'The villagers quickly agreed that it would be silly to take risks.

'That evening the square was lit with hundreds of lanterns. The Emperor had ordered a grand feast and afterwards he made a speech, saying all sorts of embarrassing things about how I had saved the village and that from now on I was to be called Tashi the Dragon Slayer. I looked over at Wise-as-an-Owl, and he gave me a little wink.

"'Now, Tashi," the Emperor went on, "you must help me to choose your prize." He beckoned me to climb up onto the podium beside him.

'There was absolute silence while everyone waited to hear what I would say. I stood there, enjoying the moment, smiling at all my dear family and friends and neighbours. How surprised they were going to be!

'"Majesty, I think the whole village should share the prize because they all helped me and stood by me on the mountainside. I have been trying to think what we might all like best." I couldn't help giving a little wiggle of excitement. "Now it might seem strange to you, Majesty, but you see, everyone has had such a wonderful week during your visit. We've all enjoyed the musicians and dancers and acrobats and play actors, and it will be so dull to go back to the old life when they are gone. So that's what we would like best – a theatre – and for your Master of Revels to send performers out here each month to entertain us and tell us stories, and give us something to look forward to."

'"*Ooh*," breathed the villagers. "That's exactly what we would like."

'The Emperor was surprised but he agreed happily enough. And so the party continued long into the night. And if the Baron and the Warlord didn't dance as joyously as the others, "Well," smiled Grandmother, "it's hard to please everyone.""

~

'Isn't that the truth?' said the waitress, who had been hovering over Tashi's shoulder ever since she'd brought the jam. 'Me, I love the opera. But my husband can't stand it. He'd rather be at home reading his book.'

'I'm with him,' said Dad. He winked at Tashi. 'Or sitting around a camp fire listening to a Tashi story.'

'Are you Tashi?' asked the waitress.

'Yes,' said Tashi.

'He comes from a land very far away,' said Jack.

'Oh, that's interesting,' said the waitress. 'How—'

'Deborah,' called the other waitress, 'could you come and take this order?'

As they all got up from the table, Dad said he didn't mind driving now as he felt so fit he could fight a dragon.

'Well,' said Deborah. 'I hope you come back very soon to tell us another story.'

'So do I,' said Jack.

'And I,' said Tashi, crossing his fingers for dragon luck.

About the Authors

When Anna Fienberg was little, her mother, Barbara, read lots of stories to her. At bedtime they would travel to secret places in the world, through books. The Tashi stories began when Barbara was telling Anna how she used to tell whoppers when she was a child. Creative fibs. Tall stories. And kids would crowd around her, dying to hear the latest tale. Together they talked about a character like Barbara – someone who told fantastic stories – and over many cups of tea they cooked up Tashi.

Read all the Tashi adventures in *There Once Was a Boy Called Tashi*, *Once Tashi Met a Dragon* and the *Tashi* series. And there's more to discover in *The Amazing Tashi Activity Book*.

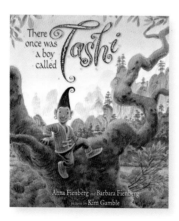